FOR MY PARENTS,
ADELE AND GEORGE

SIMON & SCHUSTER
BOOKS FOR YOUNG READERS
An imprint of Simon & Schuster Children's Publishing Division
1230 Avenue of the Americas, New York, New York 10020

Designed by Heather Wood
The text for this book is set in Raleigh Medium.
The illustrations were created with cassein paint.
Manufactured in Hong Kong by South China Printing Company (1988) Ltd.
First Edition
2 4 6 8 10 9 7 5 3 1

Library of Congress Cataloging-in-Publication Data
Greenstein, Elaine.
Mrs. Rose's garden / Elaine Greenstein.
p.   cm.
Summary: When Mrs. Rose grows a prize crop of vegetables guaranteed to win all the blue ribbons
at the County Fair, she is inspired to a generous act involving the gardens of her friends.
ISBN 0-689-80215-3
[1. Gardening—Fiction. 2. Vegetables—Fiction. 3. Contests—Fiction. 4. Sharing—Fiction.
5. Fairs—Fiction.] I. Title.
PZ7.G8517Mr 1996   [E]—dc20   95-14693

Mrs. Rose's Garden

ELAINE GREENSTEIN

SIMON & SCHUSTER BOOKS FOR YOUNG READERS

Mrs. Matilda Rose grew a vegetable garden every summer and each year she took her best vegetables to the county fair. She wanted to win a blue ribbon more than anything else in the world.

Every year Mrs. Rose tried different fertilizers and seeds to grow the biggest vegetables. Each spring she planted and waited and watched. But Mrs. Rose never won a blue ribbon. Someone else's vegetables were always larger.

One spring Mrs. Rose canceled her annual trip to visit her sister Florence and devoted all her time to her garden. She visited all four garden shops in town and bought every kind of fertilizer she could find. Mrs. Rose mixed the fertilizer together. She added her special mix to the soil when she planted the seeds. Then she watered the seeds and waited.

A few weeks later the little seedlings popped up through the soil. The plants seemed to be growing a little faster and larger than usual. Mrs. Rose was delighted.

The lettuce and the radishes were the first vegetables ready to pick. They were enormous—and all the other vegetables looked like they were going to be huge, too.

During dinner Mrs. Rose told her husband the news. "At last I'll win a blue ribbon. In fact, I'll probably win all of them!"

Mrs. Rose was so certain that she was going to win that she went to town and bought a new dress and hat to wear on her big day.

That night Mrs. Rose couldn't sleep. She tossed and turned, and finally got out of bed. She strolled through her garden. Growing these vegetables had brought her so much pleasure it seemed a shame to pick them. She'd thought it would be fun to win a blue ribbon, but now she was sure to win every single one. Somehow it didn't seem like fun anymore.

Mrs. Rose looked at the vegetables growing in her garden.

Suddenly she had an idea, a wonderful idea! She said "Good night" to her vegetables, walked back into the house, and went right to sleep.

In the morning Mrs. Rose told Mr. Rose her plan, and they got started on it right away.

They worked hard all day long and went to bed early.

The alarm clock went off at midnight, and the Roses got up. They dressed in dark clothes, got into their car, and drove to the other side of town. They parked on the street, and climbed over the fence into Hortense Splendor's garden. Very quietly Mr. Rose dug up one of Hortense's tomato plants and replaced it with one from their garden.

They put a pepper plant in Bertha Lilie's garden, and planted carrots for Harold Fulcrum. There was a cucumber plant for Doreen Starbinder, and an acorn squash for Clara Beck. Hilda Delphinium got a watermelon vine, Dr. Raymer got broccoli, and Gladys Carmel got the brussels sprouts.

Then Mr. and Mrs. Rose drove home—tired and dirty, but happy.

And everyone's garden grew and grew.

Hilda Delphinium asked Bertha Lilie if her watermelons were large this year. Bertha said, "No, but my peppers are huge."

Dr. Raymer asked Hortense Splendor if her broccoli was big this year. She said, "No larger than last year, but my tomatoes are gigantic."

Gladys Carmel asked Mrs. Rose if her brussels sprouts were the size of baseballs. Mrs. Rose said, "Oh my!"—and never answered the question.

The Roses kept their secret to themselves.

At the county fair in September, Hortense Splendor won a blue ribbon for the biggest tomato, Bertha Lilie won a blue ribbon for the biggest pepper, Harold Fulcrum won a blue ribbon for the biggest carrot, Doreen Starbinder won a blue ribbon for the biggest cucumber, Clara Beck won a blue ribbon for the biggest acorn squash, Hilda Delphinium won a blue ribbon for the biggest watermelon, Dr. Raymer won a blue ribbon for the biggest broccoli, and Gladys Carmel won a blue ribbon for the biggest brussels sprout.

And Mrs. Rose? She won the blue ribbon for growing the biggest pumpkin ever, and Mr. Rose gave Mrs. Rose a special blue ribbon for having the biggest heart.